To the Burnsides, big and small—with love
—A.M.

For Francesca Zannoni and Nik, with love and thanks
—L.V.

tiger tales
an imprint of ME Media, LLC
202 Old Ridgefield Road
Wilton, CT 06897
Published in the United States 2002
Originally published in Great Britain 2002
By Scholastic Children's Books, London
A division of Scholastic Ltd.
Text copyright ©2002 Alan MacDonald
Illustrations copyright ©2002 Louise Voce
CIP Data is available
First U.S. hardcover edition ISBN 1-58925-021-4
First U.S. paperback edition ISBN 1-58925-370-1
Printed in Dubai
1 3 5 7 9 10 8 6 4 2

Snarlyhissopus

by
Alan MacDonald

Illustrated by
Louise Voce

tiger tales

One morning, Pelican met a new animal in the jungle. She had never seen anything like it before.

"Hello," said Pelican. "What kind of animal are you?"

"I'm a hippopotamus,"
replied Hippopotamus.

Pelican flew off to tell Monkey.

"Guess what?" said Pelican. "I've seen a strange new animal."

"What is it?" asked Monkey.

Pelican tried to remember. "It's a
SPOTTYHIPPOMUS," she said.

Monkey swung off through the trees and found Zebra.

"Watch out," said Monkey. "There's a huge, ugly creature heading this way."

"What is it?" asked Zebra.

"It's a WOPPABIGAMOUSE!" said Monkey.

Zebra found Leopard
sleeping in the shade.
"Run!" said Zebra.
"There's an enormous,
slimy beast and it's
chasing me."

Leopard ran
ahead and told
Anteater.

"What's wrong?"
said Anteater fearfully.

"It's not safe! There's a hairy,
hungry, snarling monster
and I can hear it coming!"
"What is it?" asked Anteater.

"It's a
GRIPPERSNAPPERTOOTH!"
said Leopard.

Anteater told the alarming news to Giraffe. "Look out! There's a gigantic, pink jelly thing coming and it will swallow you whole!"

"What is it?" asked Giraffe, trembling at the knees.

"It's a GULPAWOBBLETUSK!"
said Anteater.

Giraffe found
Elephant taking
his nap.

"Wake up! Wake up!" panted Giraffe. "A terrible, roaring, clawing, wild-eyed monster is going to gobble us all up."

Elephant opened one eye. "What kind of monster?" he yawned.

"A SNARLYHISSOPUS!"

Elephant waggled his great ears and said *he* wasn't scared of monsters. He sent Giraffe to bring all the animals to the high hill.

"Now listen, this is my plan," said Elephant. "We'll all hide and when the monster comes we'll . . .

jump on it,

push it,

bump it,

and shove it
downhill to
the muddy
brown creek.
That will
teach it
a lesson."

All the animals
agreed this was a
clever plan and went
to find hiding places.

After a little while, they heard something moving in the bushes. The monster was coming!

On a signal from Elephant, they all
jumped on it. Pushing, bumping, and
shoving with all their might, they rolled
the monster downhill into the muddy
brown creek.

splash!

Hippopotamus rolled over in the warm, squishy mud. "Oh, lovely!" she said. Elephant stared. "But you're not a monster! Where is the SNARLYHISSOPUS?"

"I think you're a bit mixed-up," Hippopotamus giggled. "I'm a hippopotamus, and hippopotamuses love mud baths. Have you ever tried one yourself?"

None of
them had.
So they all
jumped into
the muddy
brown creek.
And before
long, it was
hard to tell
which of
them was a
hippopotamus
and which
was a . . .

WHAT-ON-EARTHAMUS!